characters created by lauren child

I am going to SAVE a panda!

Grosset & Dunlap
An Imprint of Penguin Group (USA) Inc.

Charlie ♥ and Lola™

Text based on the script
written by Bridget Hurst

Illustrations from the TV
animations produced by Tiger Aspect

GROSSET & DUNLAP
Published by the Penguin Group
Penguin Group (USA) Inc., 375 Hudson Street, New York, New York 10014, USA
Penguin Group (Canada), 90 Eglinton Avenue East, Suite 700, Toronto, Ontario M4P 2Y3, Canada
(a division of Pearson Penguin Canada Inc.)
Penguin Books Ltd., 80 Strand, London WC2R 0RL, England
Penguin Group Ireland, 25 St. Stephen's Green, Dublin 2, Ireland
(a division of Penguin Books Ltd.)
Penguin Group (Australia), 250 Camberwell Road, Camberwell, Victoria 3124, Australia
(a division of Pearson Australia Group Pty. Ltd.)
Penguin Books India Pvt. Ltd., 11 Community Centre, Panchsheel Park, New Delhi—110 017, India
Penguin Group (NZ), 67 Apollo Drive, Rosedale, North Shore 0632, New Zealand
(a division of Pearson New Zealand Ltd.)
Penguin Books (South Africa) (Pty.) Ltd., 24 Sturdee Avenue,
Rosebank, Johannesburg 2196, South Africa

Penguin Books Ltd., Registered Offices: 80 Strand, London WC2R 0RL, England

Library of Congress Cataloging-in-Publication Data is available.

ISBN 978-0-448-45328-6   10 9 8 7

I have this little sister, Lola.
She is small and very funny.
She is very excited because
it is Save an **Animal** Day at school.

On the way to school,
Lola says,
"I would be really
absolutely extremely
good at saving animals."

Lotta says,
"Maybe we can
save some giraffes!"

Lola says,
      "Yes! Sometimes,
because they are so tall,
      giraffes get their heads
stuck in the clouds."

      Lotta says,
            "Let's blow."

Lola says,
      "See? We are very good
at saving animals."

      "Yes! Very good!"
            says Lotta.

"Umm, that's not
    what it means
to save an **animal**," I say.
    "We need to raise
money to build safe homes
    for **animals**.
    That way they won't
become **extinct**."

Then Lola asks,
    "What's a stinkt?"

And I say,
"EXTINCT means
    no more of that **animal**
in the whole entire world."

And Lola says, "OH NO!"

I say, "Some people
make jewelry
from turtles' shells.

In Africa,
some people steal
rhinoceroses' horns.

And there aren't many
parrots in Mexico
because their trees are
being chopped down."

Marv says,
"These are called
endangered animals."

Lola and Lotta say,
"We definitely must help!"

At the library,
Lotta says,
　　"Look! Snowy leopards
are endangered."

　　Then Marv says,
"So are moon jellyfish."

　　I say,
"And brown pelicans."

Lola says,
　　"Oh no!
Pandas are in danger, too!"

I say,
"Giant **pandas** live in China.
        They eat bamboo
all day long."

        And Marv says,
"But people are cutting
        down all their **bamboo**."

Then I say,
"Without enough food,
        giant **pandas** might
disappear completely."

So Lola says,
        "I think I would
like to save a **panda**."

And we all say,
        "Yes!"

I say,
"Now we need sponsors.
They'll give us money
for doing difficult things,
like swimming
five laps."

Lotta says,
"But I can't swim yet."

So I ask,
"Well, what are you
good at?"

Lotta says,
"I am good at skipping
and Lola is very good
at hopping."

Later I say,
"Look at all our **sponsors**!
We're going to raise
lots of money
tomorrow."

Lola says,
"I can't wait to
hop, hop, and hop!"

"And skip, skip, and skip!"
says Lotta.

"And stand
on
one
leg!"
says Marv.

"And **balance** an
apple on my head!" I say.

The next morning,
Lola is all spotty.
She has the chicken pox.

Lola says,
"Mum says I absolutely
cannot go to school.
Now I won't be
able to do the sponsored
hopping and save
a giant panda."

So I say,
"Sorry, Lola.
I'll come back at
lunch to tell you
how everyone's doing."

At lunch I say,
"Everyone has raised
     lots of **money**."

But Lola says,
"Everyone except me."

Then I say,
     "Maybe you still can!
What if people
     sponsor your **spots**?"

Lola says,
"That is a very good idea!"

I say, "Sixty-four . . . sixty-five!
Lola, you've raised the most money!
We're definitely going to save a giant **panda** now."
And Lola says, "You haven't even seen
the **spots** on my tummy yet, Charlie!"